CLASSIC COLLECTION

THE STRANGE CASE OF
DR. JEKYLL
AND MR. HYDE

ROBERT LOUIS STEVENSON

ADAPTED BY ANNE ROONEY · ILLUSTRATED BY TOM MCGRATH

The Door

Mr. Utterson, the lawyer, was a tall, thin man who never smiled. His friends were his relatives, or those he had met by chance and known for a long time. Mr. Enfield was one of those friends, and a distant cousin, too. The two men had the habit of walking together every Sunday. On one of these Sunday walks they passed an unmarked door with peeling paint, the only entrance to a building without windows.

"I can tell you a strange story about that house," Mr. Enfield said. "A while ago I was coming home late, about three in the morning, when suddenly a man rushed around a corner and straight into a little girl. He trampled across her and kept going! I gave chase and dragged him back to where her family and a doctor had gathered. Luckily, the little girl was not badly hurt.

"You would expect the family to be angry with such a man. But it was more than anger—we all felt an overwhelming hatred toward him. Even the kindly doctor, I could see, felt repulsed by him and disgusted by his actions. He would pay for what he had done— we told him that we would shame him throughout London. He sneered, but was clearly worried.

"'All men wish to avoid a scene,' he said. 'Name your price.'

"We demanded that he pay £100 to the girl's family in return for us not telling people what had happened."

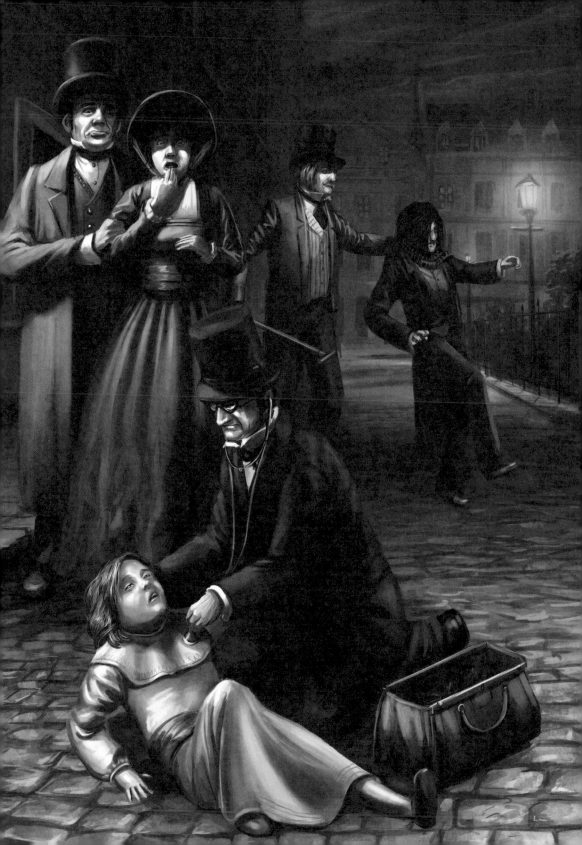

"To get the money, he brought us to this door, took out a key and let himself in. He soon returned with £10 in gold and a check signed by a famous and honorable man for £90. And there's the mystery—why would a well-respected man sign a check for such a terrible person?"

Mr. Enfield had since watched the house, and no one other than the awful man had ever gone in or out. Although the building had no windows onto the street, it did have four windows onto an inner courtyard. There was usually smoke coming from the chimney, so clearly someone was living there.

"Did you find out the name of this rogue?" Utterson asked.

"Yes. It's Hyde," Enfield answered.

"What sort of a man is he?"

"There is something wrong with his appearance, something displeasing," Enfield said. "I never saw a man I disliked so much—but I can't say exactly why."

"Are you sure he used a key?" Utterson asked. "I know it must seem a strange question, but I think I may already know whose name was on that check—the man who lives in this house is a good friend of mine."

"I see," Enfield said. "But Hyde did have a key, and does still. I saw him use it a week ago. This is a very strange business. It makes me feel uneasy—let us say no more of the matter!"

"Mr. Seek"

That night, Utterson took out the will he was keeping safe for his friend, Dr. Henry Jekyll. Utterson read over it. The will stated that if Jekyll died everything he owned should immediately pass to his friend Mr. Edward Hyde. And if Jekyll were to disappear for more than three months, Mr. Hyde should take over his belongings and life. Utterson had always thought this strange, as he had never heard of Hyde before. Now he thought it even more disturbing, as Hyde did not sound like a person Jekyll would have as a friend.

Utterson went to ask Dr. Lanyon, an old friend of Jekyll's, if he had heard of Mr. Hyde.

"No, I don't know of him and I don't see much of Jekyll anymore, either," Lanyon said. "About ten years ago, he began to behave very strangely—I believe his mind was disturbed."

The story of the horrible man who had mercilessly knocked down a child worried Utterson so much that he couldn't sleep. He wondered what Jekyll's connection to him was. His curiosity grew, and he started to hang around near the shabby door to see Hyde for himself.

"If he is Mr. Hyde, I shall be Mr. Seek," he said to himself.

Finally, one cold night, Utterson heard distant footsteps and soon saw a small man skulk toward the door. The man looked around himself shiftily as he walked.

Mr. Utterson meets Mr. Hyde

Utterson felt complete disgust at the sight of Hyde, but he stepped out of the shadows to greet him.

"Mr. Hyde, I presume?" Utterson said.

"That's my name. What do you want?" he hissed.

"I need to see Dr. Jekyll," said Utterson boldly.

"Dr. Jekyll is not here," the man replied. "How do you know who I am?"

"We have friends in common, you and I."

"Who?" Hyde asked.

"Well, Dr. Jekyll, for instance," Utterson said.

"He would not tell you about me!" Hyde said angrily, and pushed through the door, slamming it behind him.

"The man is barely human," Utterson said to himself. "If ever I saw the mark of the devil on a man, it's on Jekyll's new friend."

Utterson then went to visit Jekyll, but his friend was out. He asked Poole, his servant, about Hyde and learned that they rarely saw him in the house—he went in and out through Jekyll's laboratory door. Utterson went home, certain that Hyde must have some hold over Jekyll, perhaps threatening to reveal some secret from his past.

Two weeks later, Utterson went to dinner at Jekyll's house. When Utterson mentioned Hyde, Jekyll went pale.

"I know you've seen Hyde," Jekyll said. "He told me. Please, just promise that if I disappear, you'll see that he gets his rights as set out in my will. Now I beg you never to speak of him again!"

Murder!

A year later, a horrible murder shocked London. The only witness was a servant girl, who saw the whole thing from her window. An old man walking down the street ran into a shorter man who at first shouted at him, then the shorter man raised his walking stick and hit him with it, over and over again. As the old man fell to the ground, his attacker continued to beat him until the stick broke. The servant girl recognized the attacker as Mr. Hyde. She watched in horror as he beat the old man to death and then trampled over him. She was so upset by the violent scene that she fainted, and so did not tell the police until some time later.

When the police finally came, Hyde was long gone. But a letter in the old man's pocket led them to his lawyer, who happened to be Mr. Utterson. By now Utterson knew Hyde's address and, horrified to hear about the murder of his client, he took the police straight to where Hyde lived.

Hyde's house was in a poor, rough area, with places selling cheap food and ragged children huddling in doorways. Jekyll was well respected in his work and was reasonably wealthy, so Utterson thought it a strange place for one of his friends to live. The policeman knocked on the door, and a pale woman with silver hair and an evil glint in her eye opened it.

"Mr. Hyde is not here," she declared, smiling tightly through her thin lips. "He popped in last night for just a few minutes, but that's all. He's not been here in almost two months, really."

"We wish to see his rooms," replied Utterson. "This is Inspector Newcomen of Scotland Yard."

"Oh! He's in trouble! What has he done?" The woman seemed pleased at the thought of this, and happily let the two men inside.

"This Hyde character is obviously not popular," the police officer muttered to Utterson.

The house was large but Hyde used only two of the rooms, leaving the others empty. Utterson was surprised to see that the place was tastefully decorated, but it looked terribly messy. There were clothes spilling out of open drawers, and burned papers piled in the fireplace. It looked as if someone had been frantically searching for something and then left in a great hurry. The other half of the broken walking stick, thrown behind the door, confirmed Hyde's guilt.

Later that afternoon, Utterson went to Jekyll's house. He found Jekyll sitting in the office above his laboratory looking pale and ill—Utterson had never seen him in such a terrible state. He asked his friend if he was helping Hyde to escape the police.

"I swear I am done with Hyde!" Jekyll promised. "I'll never set eyes on him again. He has gone, gone for good. And I have learned a terrible lesson."

A Terrible Shock

Utterson was relieved at his friend's words. Then Jekyll handed him a letter.

"I don't know whether to show this to the police," he said. "Will you decide for me?"

The letter was from Hyde, and said that he had a guaranteed way to escape and would not be coming back. Jekyll said it had been hand-delivered and he had burned the envelope but, when Utterson asked Poole, he said no one had been there to deliver the letter. Fear stirred again in Utterson's heart.

That evening, Utterson sat talking with his clerk, Mr. Guest. Guest was excellent at reading a person's character in their handwriting, so Utterson showed him Hyde's letter. At that moment, a servant brought in a note from Jekyll inviting Utterson to dinner. Guest asked to see this letter, too. It was very strange—Hyde's handwriting was just like Jekyll's, but slanted backward. Utterson felt a chill creep over him—surely Jekyll was not faking notes for a murderer?

For two months, all was well. Jekyll was his old self, dining with friends and working. But then for several days in a row he said he was too ill to see Utterson.

Utterson went to see Lanyon, but was shocked at the change in him. Lanyon had suddenly become thin and ill and he told Utterson he was dying.

"I have had a terrible shock that I shall never recover from," he said. "I have only a few more weeks to live . . ."

The Quarrel with Dr. Lanyon

"Our friend Jekyll is also ill," Utterson remarked.
"Never speak of him to me!" Lanyon said.
"I am finished with him forever—he is dead to me!
When I die, you might learn the right and wrong of
this matter but, for now, I dare not tell you."

When Utterson got home, he wrote to Jekyll asking
why he and Lanyon were no longer friends. He received
a long reply the next day, saying the quarrel was final
and Jekyll had no intention of ever speaking to Lanyon
again. Jekyll added that although he still considered
Utterson to be his friend, he could not see him either.

"I mean now to lead a secluded life. I have brought
a terrible fate upon myself. I could never have imagined
that the world could contain such suffering and terror."

Utterson read the letter in astonishment. Had his
friend gone mad? He felt hurt, but there was nothing
he could do. A week later, Lanyon's health became
worse and, within another week, he died. After the
funeral, Utterson found an envelope addressed to him
from Lanyon with the instruction that it should only be
opened in the event of Jekyll's death or disappearance.

The reference again to Jekyll's disappearance chilled
Utterson to the bone. Why did Jekyll think he might
disappear? Utterson was desperate to know more, but
he respected Lanyon's wishes. With a trembling hand,
he put the unopened envelope in his safe alongside
Jekyll's will.

A Face at the Window

Some time later, Utterson was taking his regular Sunday walk with Enfield when they stopped in front of the same door that had started Enfield's story long before.

"That's the last we will hear of Hyde," Enfield said.

"I do hope so," Utterson replied. "I saw him once and also felt the horror you described."

"It would be impossible not to feel that way," Enfield replied. "I should tell you that I do know that this door is the back entrance to Dr. Jekyll's laboratory."

"Ah, well, now that you know who lives here," Utterson replied, "we may as well step through into the courtyard and take a look. I am worried about Jekyll."

They walked through and looked up to the window of Jekyll's office, which was above his laboratory. There they saw him, sitting by the window, looking miserable.

Utterson called up to him, introducing his cousin and inviting Jekyll to walk with them.

"I would like to," Jekyll replied, "but it is impossible."

"Then stay and talk with us through the window," Utterson suggested. Jekyll agreed but, a moment later, such a look of utter terror and despair crossed his face

that Utterson's blood ran cold. Jekyll slammed the window shut. Horrified, and not knowing what had happened, Utterson and Enfield walked away. They dared not speak until they were some distance away.

"God forgive us!" Utterson said.

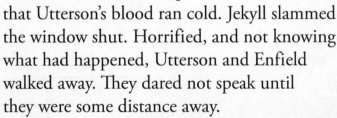

A Strange Development

Some time later, Utterson was sitting at home on a cold night in March when Poole, Jekyll's butler, arrived at the house. The man was in a terrible state. He was pale and frightened, and could hardly speak.

"Mr. Utterson, sir," he stammered, "there is something wrong. I've been afraid for the past week, and I can bear it no more. I think there's been foul play!"

Utterson could get no more from him, and so at last offered to go with him to Jekyll's house.

When they got there, Poole looked more terrified than ever. Inside, all the servants were gathered together in the hallway, and one maid cried openly. Poole silenced her, called for a candle and took Utterson into the garden. They crossed the courtyard to Jekyll's laboratory. Poole told Utterson to stand and listen, and not to enter Jekyll's office even if invited in. Then he knocked on the door and announced that Utterson had come to visit.

"Tell him I cannot see anyone!" a voice answered.

"Do you think that sounds like my master's voice?" Poole asked quietly.

"It is much changed," Utterson admitted nervously.

"I don't think it's him," Poole said. "I fear that he has been murdered! I think he was killed eight days ago, when we heard him cry out upon the name of God. Whoever or whatever is in there instead of him, and why they stay there—that's a mystery, sir."

Utterson found Poole's theory hard to believe and asked him what evidence he had.

"All week," Poole replied, "whoever, or whatever, is in there has been crying out for medicine that they can't seem to get. I find notes on the stairs to take to the pharmacy, but everything I bring back is rejected. Look."

Poole showed Utterson a note to a pharmacist, asking for medicine and saying that the batches that had been sent in the past were no good.

"Have you seen Jekyll?" Utterson asked. Poole said that he had seen him from a distance in the laboratory, but that when Jekyll had spotted Poole he had cried out and hurried away. He had been wearing a mask to hide his face.

"Well," Utterson said, "it's clear that your master has an illness that has caused a deformity and also tortures his mind. The only explanation can be that he is searching for this medicine to cure himself. I only hope that he finds this medicine soon."

But Poole wasn't satisfied. "I don't think it *was* my master, though," he said. "My master is a tall man, and the person that ran from me was almost a dwarf. That person in the mask, whoever it was, wasn't Dr. Jekyll. I think my poor master has been murdered!"

"If you think that," Utterson said, "then we must find out for sure. It is my duty to break down the door and prove he is alive!"

A Shocking Discovery

Utterson picked up a poker and Poole an ax, preparing themselves to smash through the door to Jekyll's office.

"Poole, if you have any suspicions about what, or who, we might find, speak now," said Utterson.

"Sir, I think it might be Hyde," Poole said. "He still had a key to the laboratory when he disappeared after the murder. He has an unnatural way about him that chills your bones. As that thing ran past me, I felt the same thrill of horror. I know that's not proof, but I feel almost certain it's Hyde."

They called a footman to wait by the back door, in case anyone tried to escape that way, and waited a while, listening to the sound of pacing feet.

"It's all he does," Poole said, "day and night. Though once I heard him weeping and it sent such a chill of horror through me that I could have wept myself."

Utterson called out, demanding to see Jekyll and saying they would break in if he did not open the door.

"For God's sake, have mercy!" came the reply.

"That's not Jekyll's voice—it's Hyde's!" Utterson cried. "Down with the door!"

Poole swung the ax and the blow shook the building. They heard a terrified cry from inside the room. He struck again and again, the wood splintering with the blows, until at last the door gave way and the two men stumbled into the room.

It looked like any tidy London room, with a fire burning in the fireplace and things set out ready for tea nearby. Papers were neatly ordered on the desk. But in the middle of the room, the twisted body of a man lay face down on the floor. He was still twitching as Utterson and Poole came close. He was small in size and dressed in clothes much too large for him. Turning him on his back, they saw Hyde's face. He was dead, and the smell of almonds told Utterson that he'd poisoned himself with arsenic.

"We are too late," Utterson groaned. "All that remains now is to find your master's body. We must find Jekyll."

They searched the laboratory downstairs, and all the closets and cupboards. The cellar door opened onto a curtain of cobwebs that had not been disturbed in years, so they knew that it was empty. There was no sign of Jekyll anywhere, dead or alive.

They started looking around the office again for clues. One table showed signs of chemical experiments, with glass dishes of the powder that Poole had fetched from the pharmacy. The mirror was angled to the ceiling, so that it did not reflect anything in the room. It was as though someone had been worried about what their reflection might reveal. Among the papers on the desk, they found an envelope addressed to Utterson. The lawyer opened it, fumbling in his haste, and several items fell out.

Dr. Jekyll's Will

One of the items was Jekyll's new will, which named Utterson as his heir instead of Hyde. Utterson was astonished. What could this mean?

"This will has been here all along. Hyde could easily have destroyed it!" he said. Then he picked up a note written in Jekyll's handwriting, dated that same day.

"Poole," he said, "he was here today! He can't have been killed and disposed of so quickly—he must have gone away. And, if he was here so recently, how can we be sure that he did not kill Hyde?"

"Go ahead and read it, sir," Poole said.

"I am terrified of what I might discover," Utterson said in a low voice. But, with his heart pounding in his chest, he opened the letter:

My dear Utterson, if you are reading this I have disappeared. I don't know how or why, but I fear the end is near. Go first and read the document that Lanyon gave you. Then read my confession enclosed here.

Utterson picked up the sealed confession.

"It is now ten o'clock. I will go home," Utterson said, "to read both documents in peace. But I will come back before midnight and we will send for the police."

They left Hyde's body where they had found it, and locked up the laboratory. With a feeling of dread, Utterson walked home. Who knew what Jekyll's confession and the envelope from Lanyon would reveal?

Dr. Lanyon's Letter

Utterson stood by the fire to read the letter from Lanyon:

On January 9th, I received a letter from Dr. Jekyll, sent by registered delivery to arrive the same night. I had only dined with Jekyll the day before, and was surprised he would have such urgent news to share. It held a strange request: to go straight to Jekyll's house, where Poole would be waiting with a locksmith to help me break into the office. I was to fetch a drawer from a cabinet containing some powders, a small bottle of liquid and a book. Then I was to wait at home until midnight, when a man would come to collect it, giving Jekyll's name. This must be done in secret, with none of my servants seeing the man. The letter said that if I failed in this task, Jekyll would soon be dead or mad.

I was sure Jekyll must be mad already to send such a letter, but thought it best to do as he asked. I went to his house, where Poole was indeed waiting, and with much difficulty we broke into the office. I took the drawer home and examined it. The powders were small white crystals, like salt. The glass bottle held a strong-smelling red liquid. The book was a simple notebook showing a list of dates, going back over several years, and beside some of them the word "double" was written. I sent my servants to bed, loaded my revolver, and settled down to wait.

No sooner did the clock strike midnight than there was a tap at the door. I opened it and found a small man shrinking into the shadows.

"Did Dr. Jekyll send you?" I asked, and he nodded. I invited him in. When I saw him in the light, the man filled me with an odd mixture of disgust and curiosity. Something about him was terribly shocking. His clothes were far too large for him, the pants and sleeves rolled up and the collar gaping open. But, instead of looking comical, his outfit added to the horror. He grabbed my arm urgently.

"Have you got it?" he hissed.

His touch chilled my blood, and I shook him off.

"Please don't do that," I said.

He sat down and apologized, but was clearly very agitated and only just able to keep himself under control. I pointed to the drawer, which I had put on the floor. He ran to it, snatched it up and gave a sob of relief when he saw the contents.

"Do you have a glass?" he asked.

With a trembling hand, I passed him a tumbler. He measured out a small amount of the red liquid, and then added one of the powders. The mixture fizzed dramatically and smoke billowed up into the air. It turned first a deep purple, and then a vivid green. The man put the glass to his lips, about to drink greedily. Then, quite suddenly, he stopped dead in his tracks and turned to face me . . .

"Will you be wise and let me drink this in the street?" he said. "Or are you too curious? It will be as you choose. You can remain in your present state, happy to have done an act of kindness for an old friend. Otherwise, your eyes are about to be opened to a knowledge that would astonish even the devil himself."

I pretended to be calm, but didn't feel it.

"I have gone a long way into this strange business," I said. "I'll see it through."

"As you wish, Lanyon. You have never believed in strange and supernatural things, but that is about to change."

He tipped the glass and drank the liquid in one gulp, then staggered and clutched at the table. His mouth was open, his eyes staring. I watched in horror. His face seemed to swell and grow darker, his features to melt and move. I jumped backward, flattening myself against the wall and cried out in alarm.

There, before me, stood Dr. Jekyll. He was pale, shaking, and looked as if he had come back from the dead. I can't bring myself to repeat to you what he told me that evening. But I know what I saw. I can't describe the horror and shock of it all and I can't put it from my mind. I know I will now die with this secret. The creature that crept into my house that night was without a doubt Hyde, so Jekyll and Hyde are one and the same being!

Dr. Jekyll's Confession

Utterson sat down in shock, Lanyon's letter gripped tightly in his shaking hands. Had Lanyon lost his mind? He turned to pick up Jekyll's own confession, the sealed document he had left in his office. Surely this letter would reveal the truth of the matter? Utterson began to read:

I was born into a wealthy family, but had a natural urge to work hard. I wanted to impress people and that always made me reluctant to look like I was enjoying myself in case people didn't take me seriously. This meant I kept the two parts of myself separate. The greater part was the hard-working, serious part. I hid the part that enjoyed pleasure, finding it shameful. So I became something like two people in one body. I became fascinated by this idea— of a good and a bad part in a person.

I developed a potion that I thought might release the shameful part of myself, setting him free from the part that stopped me from feeling pleasure. For a long time I did not drink it, but eventually my curiosity got the better of me.

Late one night, I locked the door and drank the mixture. I was immediately tormented by pain and sickness, and a shock as great as birth or death hit my body. But it eventually passed and, when it did, I felt so alive! I went from my office to my bedroom to look in the mirror and staring back at me, for the first time, I saw the hideous face of Hyde.

I felt no horror at his ugliness, but welcomed him—recognizing him as a part of myself. The next test was to find out whether I could return to my usual self. I took another measure of the potion and suffered the same agonies. Thankfully the medicine also worked in reverse and I was transformed back to the form of Jekyll. The experiment had worked.

Hyde was smaller than me, and younger—I hoped that was because the evil part of me was smaller than the good and hadn't had a chance to develop. I noticed, too, that no one else could look at Hyde without horror. I decided it was because most people are a mix of good and evil, while Hyde was pure evil.

For a long time, I enjoyed the freedom of switching between my identities. Mostly, I was the respectable doctor and went about my business as usual. But whenever I wished, I could take the potion and become Hyde, go into town to enjoy any pleasures I chose, knowing it would never reflect badly on Jekyll. To make life easier, I told my servants that Hyde must be allowed to come and go. I rented rooms for him and decorated them. I opened a bank account in his name and learned to slant my handwriting. There were a few times when the potion didn't work, when I was unable to transform into Hyde, but that didn't greatly worry me.

Losing Control

*T*hen, one day, I had a terrible shock. I awoke in the morning feeling like I was in the wrong place, yet I was still in my house. It was only when I looked down and saw Hyde's hand lying on the sheet that I realized what had happened.

Although I had gone to bed as Jekyll, I'd woken up as Hyde. The change had happened without the potion! I was filled with horror and dread.

At first, it had been difficult to transform into the shape of Hyde, but now it was impossible to keep him away! He was gaining the upper hand. I rushed to the laboratory to find the potion, startling one of the servants, and took it immediately. I went down to breakfast as Jekyll that day, though I did not really feel like eating.

I felt then that I had to choose between being Jekyll or Hyde. It was a hard decision for me to make. Jekyll always remembered and enjoyed Hyde's early excursions, but Hyde took no notice at all of Jekyll's life. If I gave up Jekyll, I would lose my work and my reputation. Not to mention my friends and everything I valued. But, if I gave up Hyde, I would lose the freedom to enjoy pleasure without fear of the consequences.

In the end, I chose to remain in the shape of Jekyll. For two months I didn't touch the potion at all. But then I started to long for Hyde's freedom. I couldn't wait any longer—I fetched a dose of the potion and drank it down thirstily.

After two months without it, the potion's effect was powerful. My devil had been caged for too long; the spirit of hell awoke in me and raged. As Hyde, I went out into the street, impatient for evil pleasures. I found an old man and beat him to death with terrible glee.

But even Hyde was aware of the danger the crime brought. He ran to my laboratory and took the potion immediately. In Jekyll's form, he suffered no punishment. I felt terrible guilt and shame, but knew I must remain as Jekyll. That was a relief—the choice had been made for me. If Hyde ever showed his face again he would be hanged for his crimes.

My relief did not last long. One clear January day I was walking in Regent's Park and had stopped to sit down on a bench. No sooner had I thought that I was now back to being the same as other men, with good and evil parts in one body, than I felt terribly sick and shaky. The feeling passed, but when I looked down at my hands and clothes, it was Hyde's body I saw. Aware of the danger of being caught as the murderer, even by my own servants if he went home, Hyde went to a hotel, but he had to get the potion, which was in my office. He wrote letters in my handwriting to both Poole and Lanyon, arranging a way for Lanyon to get the potion and Hyde to collect it from him.

The Last Night

When night fell, Hyde took a cab and rode around and around. Then he walked, keeping to the shadows. He was haunted by his fears, muttering to himself and striking out at anyone who spoke to him. At last he went to Lanyon's house and took the potion. I am sorry for horrifying my old friend, but that is only a tiny drop in the terrors of that night.

It was no longer fear of hanging that drove me, but fear of being Hyde. I went home and slept, relieved to wake as Jekyll, and be near my potions. But as I crossed the courtyard I felt the shaking and sickness of the coming change again. I rushed to my office, but it took a double dose of the potion to return me to myself.

Six hours later, the change came yet again. It was happening more and more frequently and it no longer felt like something I could control. From that day on I struggled constantly to remain as Jekyll, taking the potion almost all the time. If I slept, I woke as Hyde, and so I slept very little and soon became exhausted.

The pains of the transition grew less, until I slipped quite easily between the two forms. Hyde grew stronger; now he raged with murderous desires and hatred. He knew he could only escape punishment for his crimes in the body of Jekyll. His anger over this led him to destroy all of my books and the portrait of my father. But his love of life is wonderful, and he fears my power to end his life. For that, I almost pity him.

But it all came to an end. I have finally run out of the salt I need to make the potion. I have sent again and again for it, but I can't get hold of the same salt. I have drunk other potions but they have no effect. It's clear now that the first batch was impure, and it was the impurity that made it work – but I don't know what the impurity was. So I have no more potion. When I next turn into Hyde, there will be no way to turn back. I am writing this confession now, so that it is out of the way before the change occurs. I do not want Hyde to destroy it.

Half an hour from now, I will again take on that hated personality. I will walk up and down this room – the only place of safety for Hyde – and tremble at every sound. I don't know whether Hyde will die on the gallows or will take his own life, and I don't care.

This is my true hour of death. As I lay down my pen and seal up this confession, I bring the life of that unhappy Henry Jekyll to an end.

Utterson laid the confession on his desk. A chill had crept through his body as he read the letters and he shuddered. He thanked God that Jekyll had been released from his living nightmare. He then vowed to himself never to reveal the horrors of the terrible secret his friend had taken to his grave . . .

About the Author

Born in Scotland in 1850, Robert Louis Stevenson was a
sickly child. He was very thin and frail, and he suffered from
coughs and fevers throughout his life. Stevenson wanted
to be a writer from an early age and had no interest
in the family lighthouse business. He often traveled abroad,
usually for health reasons, and his journeys gave him ideas
for his stories. He published his first book at the age of 28,
and became a celebrity during his life when stories such as
Treasure Island, Kidnapped, and *The Strange Case of Dr Jekyll
and Mr Hyde* were released to his fans.
He died in Samoa in 1894.

QEB Project Editor: Tasha Percy
Editorial Director: Victoria Garrard
Art Director: Laura Roberts-Jensen
Editor: Louise John
Designer: Rachel Clark

Published in the United States by
QEB Publishing, Inc.
6 Orchard
Lake Forest, CA 92630

www.qed-publishing.co.uk

A CIP record for this book is available from the Library of Congress.

ISBN 978 1 60992 737 0

Printed in China